THE WONDERFUL WIZARD OF OZ

VOL. 5

ADAPTED FROM THE NOVEL BY L. FRANK BAUM

Writer: ERIC SHANOWER
Artist: SKOTTIE YOUNG
Colorist: JEAN-FRANCOIS BEAULIEU
Letterer: JEFF ECKLEBERRY

Assistant Editors: LAUREN SANKOVITCH & LAUREN HENRY
Associate Editor: NATE COSBY
Senior Editor: RALPH MACCHIO

Special Thanks to Chris Allo, Rich Ginter, Jeff Suter & Jim Nausedas
Collection Editor: MARK D. BEAZLEY
Assistant Editors: NELSON RIBEIRO & ALEX STARBUCK
Editor, Special Projects: JENNIFER GRÜNWALD
Senior Editor, Special Projects: JEFF YOUNGQUIST
SVP of Print & Digital Publishing Sales: DAVID GABRIEL
Production: JERRY KALINOWSKI
Book Design: SPRING HOTELING

Editor in Chief: AXEL ALONSO
Chief Creative Officer: JOE QUESADA
Publisher: DAN BUCKLEY
Executive Producer: ALAN FINE

MARVEL

visit us at www.abdopublishing.com

Reinforced library bound edition published in 2014 by Spotlight, a division of the ABDO Group, PO Box 398166, Minneapolis, Minnesota 55439. Spotlight produces high-quality reinforced library bound editions for schools and libraries. Published by agreement with Marvel Characters, Inc.

Printed in the United States of America, North Mankato, Minnesota.
102013
012014
This book contains at least 10% recycled materials.

Marvel.com

Library of Congress Cataloging-in-Publication Data

Shanower, Eric.
  The wonderful Wizard of Oz / adapted from the novel by L. Frank Baum ; writer: Eric Shanower ; artist: Skottie Young. -- Reinforced library bound edition.
     pages cm
  "Marvel."
  Summary: An eight-volume, graphic novel adaptation of L. Frank Baum's tales of Dorothy, a little girl from Kansas who is blown by a storm to the magical land of Oz, where she has amazing adventures while trying to get home.
  ISBN 978-1-61479-226-0 (vol. 1) -- ISBN 978-1-61479-227-7 (vol. 2) -- ISBN 978-1-61479-228-4 (vol. 3) -- ISBN 978-1-61479-229-1 (vol. 4) -- ISBN 978-1-61479-230-7 (vol. 5) -- ISBN 978-1-61479-231-4 (vol. 6) -- ISBN 978-1-61479-232-1 (vol. 7) -- ISBN 978-1-61479-233-8 (vol. 8)
  1. Graphic novels. [1. Graphic novels. 2. Fantasy.] I. Young, Skottie, illustrator. II. Baum, L. Frank (Lyman Frank), 1856-1919. III. Title.
  PZ7.7.S453Won 2014
  741.5'973--dc23
                                    2013029128

All Spotlight books are reinforced library binding and manufactured in the United States of America.

DAYLIGHT--

THE SOLDIER WITH THE GREEN WHISKERS LED THEM THROUGH THE STREETS OF THE EMERALD CITY.

WHICH ROAD LEADS TO THE WICKED WITCH OF THE WEST?

THERE IS NO ROAD. NO ONE EVER WISHES TO GO THAT WAY.

THEN HOW ARE WE TO FIND HER?

THAT WILL BE EASY. WHEN SHE KNOWS YOU ARE IN THE COUNTRY OF THE WINKIES, WHERE SHE RULES, SHE'LL FIND YOU AND MAKE YOU ALL HER SLAVES.

PERHAPS NOT, FOR WE MEAN TO DESTROY HER.

OH, THAT'S DIFFERENT. NO ONE HAS EVER DESTROYED HER BEFORE, SO I NATURALLY THOUGHT SHE'D MAKE SLAVES OF YOU, AS SHE HAS ALL OF THE REST.

BUT TAKE CARE -- SHE'S WICKED AND FIERCE, AND MAY NOT ALLOW YOU TO DESTROY HER.

KEEP TO THE WEST, WHERE THE SUN SETS, AND YOU CANNOT FAIL TO FIND HER.

*T*HE EMERALD CITY WAS SOON LEFT FAR BEHIND. IN THE AFTERNOON THE SUN SHONE HOT IN THEIR FACES.

BEFORE NIGHT DOROTHY AND TOTO AND THE LION WERE TIRED, AND LAY DOWN UPON THE GRASS AND FELL ASLEEP.

NOW, THE WICKED WITCH OF THE WEST HAD BUT ONE EYE.

Yet that eye was as powerful as a telescope and could see everywhere.

She saw Dorothy lying asleep, with her friends all around her.

They were a long distance off, but the Wicked Witch was angry to find them in her country.

WEEET!

Go to those people and tear them to pieces!

Aren't you going to make them your slaves?

NO, ONE IS OF TIN, AND ONE OF STRAW -- ONE IS A GIRL AND ANOTHER A LION. NONE OF THEM IS FIT TO WORK.

VERY WELL.

THE SCARECROW AND THE WOODMAN HEARD THE WOLVES COMING.

THIS IS MY FIGHT, SO GET BEHIND ME AND I'LL MEET THEM AS THEY COME.

THERE WERE FORTY WOLVES, AND FORTY TIMES A WOLF WAS KILLED, SO THAT AT LAST THEY ALL LAY DEAD.

THANK YOU FOR SAVING US.

*T*HE WICKED WITCH WAS ANGRIER THAN BEFORE.

FLY AT ONCE TO THE STRANGERS.

FWEET! FWEET!

PECK OUT THEIR EYES AND TEAR THEM TO PIECES!

THIS IS MY BATTLE, SO LIE DOWN BESIDE ME AND YOU WILL NOT BE HARMED.

THERE WERE FORTY CROWS, AND FORTY TIMES THE SCARECROW TWISTED A NECK, UNTIL AT LAST ALL WERE LYING DEAD.

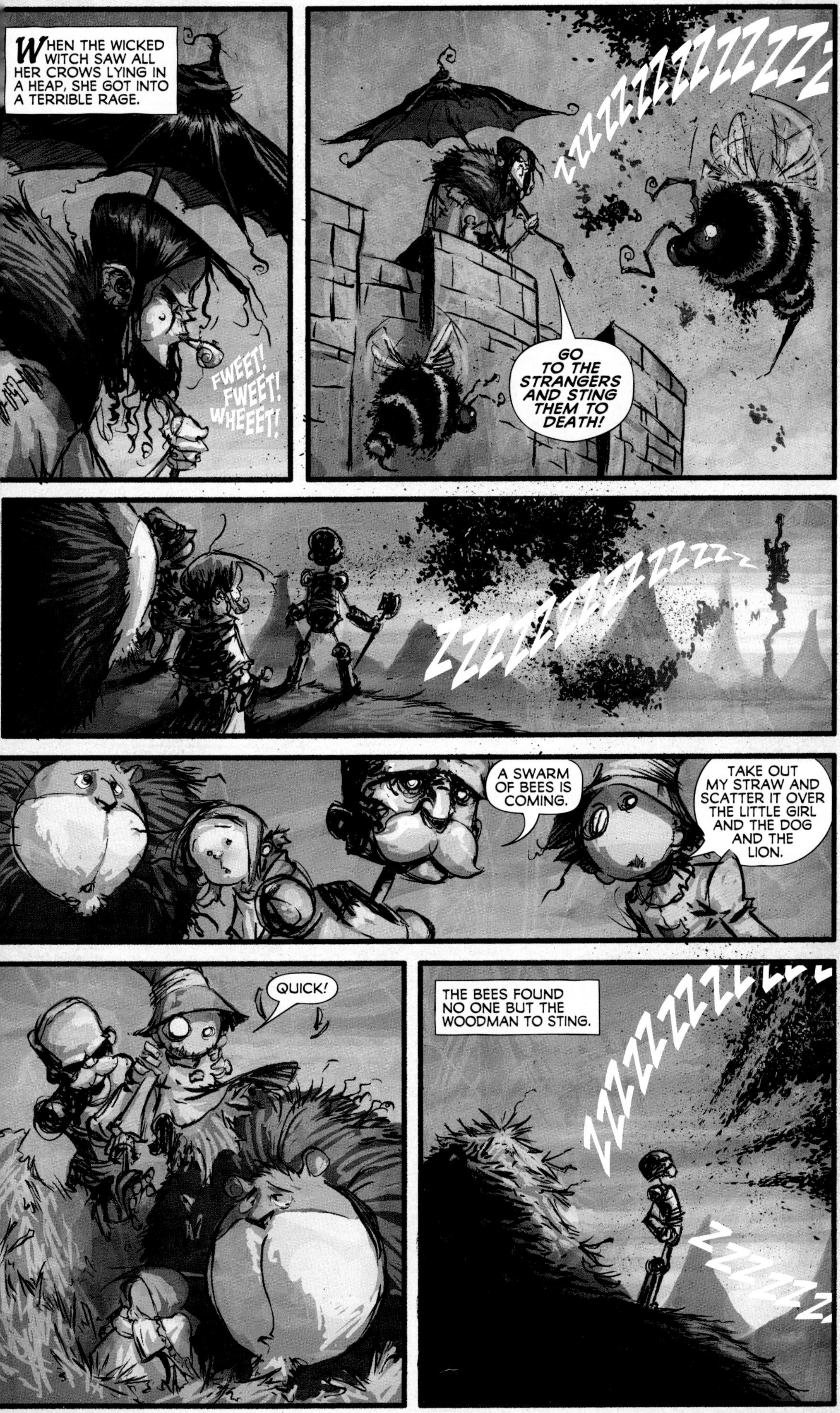
WHEN THE WICKED WITCH SAW ALL HER CROWS LYING IN A HEAP, SHE GOT INTO A TERRIBLE RAGE.
FWEET! FWEET! WHEEET!
ZZZZZZZZZZZZZZZZ
GO TO THE STRANGERS AND STING THEM TO DEATH!
ZZZZZZZZZZZZZZZZZ
A SWARM OF BEES IS COMING.
TAKE OUT MY STRAW AND SCATTER IT OVER THE LITTLE GIRL AND THE DOG AND THE LION.
QUICK!
THE BEES FOUND NO ONE BUT THE WOODMAN TO STING.
ZZZZZZZZZZZZZ
ZZZZZ

So They flew at him and broke off all their stings.

As bees cannot live when their stings are broken, that was the end of the black bees.

YAAH!

The wicked witch called a dozen of her slaves, who were the Winkies.

GO TO THE STRANGERS AND DESTROY THEM!

The Winkies were not a brave people.

RROOOAAARR!

*T*HEY RAN BACK AS FAST AS THEY COULD.

BACK TO YOUR WORK!

THE WITCH COULD NOT UNDERSTAND HOW ALL HER PLANS TO DESTROY THE STRANGERS HAD FAILED.

IN HER CUPBOARD WAS A GOLDEN CAP. WHOEVER OWNED IT COULD CALL THREE TIMES -- AND NO MORE --

-- UPON THE WINGED MONKEYS, WHO WOULD OBEY ANY ORDERS THEY WERE GIVEN.

TWICE ALREADY THE WICKED WITCH HAD USED THE CHARM OF THE CAP. ONCE WAS WHEN SHE'D MADE THE WINKIES HER SLAVES, AND SET HERSELF TO RULE OVER THEIR COUNTRY.

THE SECOND TIME WAS WHEN SHE'D FOUGHT AGAINST THE GREAT OZ HIMSELF, AND DRIVEN HIM OUT OF THE LAND OF THE WEST.

ONLY ONCE MORE COULD SHE USE THE GOLDEN CAP.

NOW THAT MY WOLVES AND CROWS AND BEES ARE GONE, AND MY SLAVES SCARED AWAY, THERE IS ONLY ONE WAY LEFT TO DESTROY THE STRANGERS.

EP-PE, PEP-PE, KAK-KE!

HIL-LO, HOL-LO, HEL-LO!

ZIZ-ZY, ZUZ-ZY, ZIK!

RRRRUMMBLE

EEE-EEE!

OO-OOOH!!

YOU'VE CALLED US FOR THE THIRD AND LAST TIME. WHAT DO YOU COMMAND?

GO TO THE STRANGERS WHO ARE WITHIN MY LAND AND DESTROY THEM, ALL EXCEPT THE LION.

BRING THAT BEAST TO ME, FOR I HAVE A MIND TO HARNESS HIM AND MAKE HIM WORK.

YOUR COMMANDS SHALL BE OBEYED.

AA-AA-AH!!

FLAP

FLAP

OO-OOOH!

FLUTTER

EE-EEE!

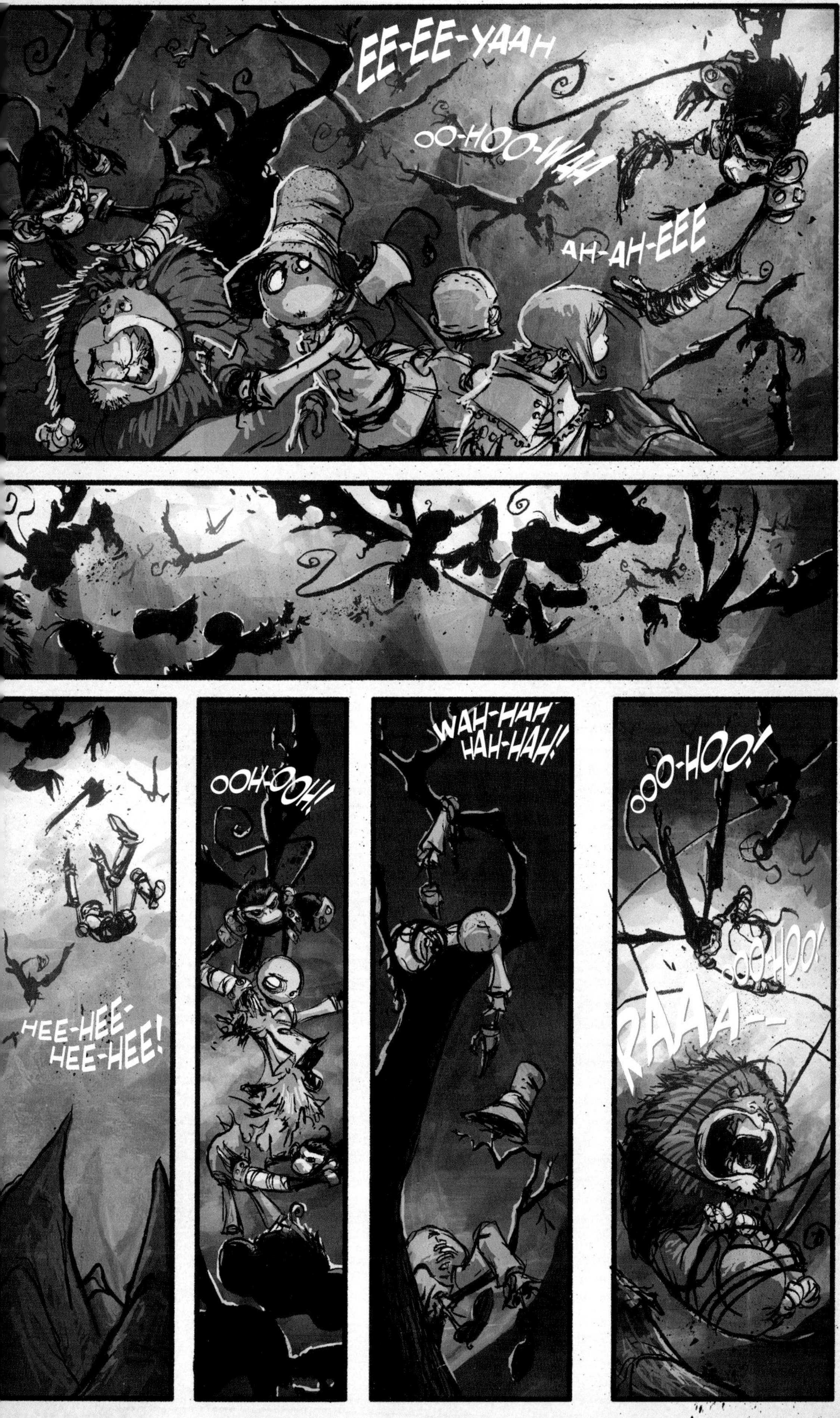
EE-EE-YAAH
OO-HOO-WAA
AH-AH-EEE
HEE-HEE-
HEE-HEE!
OOH-OOH!
WAH-HAH
HAH-HAH!
OOO-HOO!
OO-HOO!
RAAA--

EE-EE-
HAAH

OOH-
OOH

HEE-HEE-
EEE

HAAAA --

The LEADER OF THE WINGED MONKEYS SAW THE GOOD WITCH'S KISS UPON DOROTHY'S FOREHEAD.

OOH!

WE DARE NOT HARM THIS LITTLE GIRL. ALL WE CAN DO IS CARRY HER TO THE CASTLE OF THE WICKED WITCH AND LEAVE HER THERE.

WE'VE OBEYED YOU AS FAR AS WE WERE ABLE. THE TIN WOODMAN AND THE SCARECROW ARE DESTROYED, AND THE LION IS TIED UP IN YOUR YARD.

THE LITTLE GIRL WE DARE NOT HARM, NOR THE ANIMAL SHE CARRIES IN HER ARMS.

YOUR POWER OVER OUR BAND IS NOW ENDED, AND YOU'LL NEVER SEE US AGAIN.

THE WICKED WITCH SAW THE MARK ON DOROTHY'S FOREHEAD, AND KNEW THAT SHE DARE NOT HURT THE GIRL. WHEN SHE SAW THE SILVER SHOES SHE WAS TEMPTED TO RUN AWAY.

BUT SHE SAW THAT THE LITTLE GIRL DIDN'T KNOW OF THE WONDERFUL POWER THE SHOES GAVE HER.

HA! I CAN STILL MAKE HER MY SLAVE, FOR SHE DOESN'T KNOW HOW TO USE HER POWER.

COME WITH ME, AND SEE THAT YOU MIND EVERYTHING I TELL YOU, FOR IF YOU DON'T I'LL MAKE AN END OF YOU.

CLEAN THE POTS AND KETTLES AND SWEEP THE FLOOR AND KEEP THE FIRE FED WITH WOOD -- OR I SHALL BEAT YOU!

LIKE *THIS!*

RRR

*T*HE WITCH DID NOT BLEED, FOR SHE WAS SO WICKED THAT THE BLOOD IN HER HAD DRIED UP.

LET THAT ANIMAL APPROACH ME AGAI AND I SHALL BEAT YOU BOTH SEVERELY!

BUT IN TRUTH, SHE DIDN'T DARE TO STRIKE DOROTHY, BECAUSE OF THE MARK UPON THE GIRL'S FOREHEAD.

DOROTHY WENT TO WORK MEEKLY, WITH HER MIND MADE UP TO WORK AS HARD AS SHE COULD, FOR SHE WAS GLAD THE WICKED WITCH HAD DECIDED NOT TO KILL HER.

THE WITCH THOUGHT SHE WOULD HARNESS THE COWARDLY LION.

IT WILL AMUSE ME, I'M SURE, TO MAKE HIM DRAW MY CHARIOT WHENEVER I WISH TO GO FOR A DRIVE.

RRRAAAAHHHH

IF I CANNOT HARNESS YOU, I CAN STARVE YOU. YOU SHALL HAVE NOTHING TO EAT UNTIL YOU DO AS I WISH.

*E*VERY DAY THE WITCH CAME TO THE GATE AT NOON.

ARE YOU READY TO BE HARNESSED?

NO. IF YOU COME IN THIS YARD I'LL BITE YOU.

THE REASON THE LION DIDN'T HAVE TO DO AS THE WITCH WISHED WAS THAT EVERY NIGHT DOROTHY CARRIED HIM FOOD.

IF WE COULD ONLY PLAN SOME WAY TO ESCAPE.

I CAN FIND NO WAY TO GET OUT OF THE CASTLE, FOR IT'S CONSTANTLY GUARDED BY THE WINKIES.

THEY'RE TOO AFRAID OF HER NOT TO DO AS SHE TELLS THEM.

DOROTHY GREW TO UNDERSTAND THAT IT WOULD BE HARDER THAN EVER TO GET BACK TO KANSAS AND AUNT EM AGAIN.

MY BEES AND CROWS AND WOLVES ARE LYING IN HEAPS, AND I'VE USED UP THE POWER OF THE GOLDEN CAP.

BUT THE SILVER SHOES WOULD GIVE ME MORE POWER THAN ALL THE OTHER THINGS I'VE LOST.

*T*HE WICKED WITCH WATCHED DOROTHY CAREFULLY, THINKING SHE MIGHT STEAL THE SHOES.

BUT THE CHILD NEVER TOOK THEM OFF EXCEPT AT NIGHT AND WHEN SHE TOOK HER BATH.

THE WITCH WAS TOO MUCH AFRAID OF THE DARK TO DARE GO IN DOROTHY'S ROOM AT NIGHT TO TAKE THE SHOES...

...AND HER DREAD OF WATER WAS GREATER THAN HER FEAR OF THE DARK. INDEED, THE OLD WITCH NEVER TOUCHED WATER, NOR EVER LET WATER TOUCH HER IN ANY WAY.

BUT THE WICKED CREATURE WAS VERY CUNNING, AND SHE FINALLY THOUGHT OF A TRICK THAT WOULD GIVE HER WHAT SHE WANTED.

SHE PLACED A BAR OF IRON ON THE FLOOR...

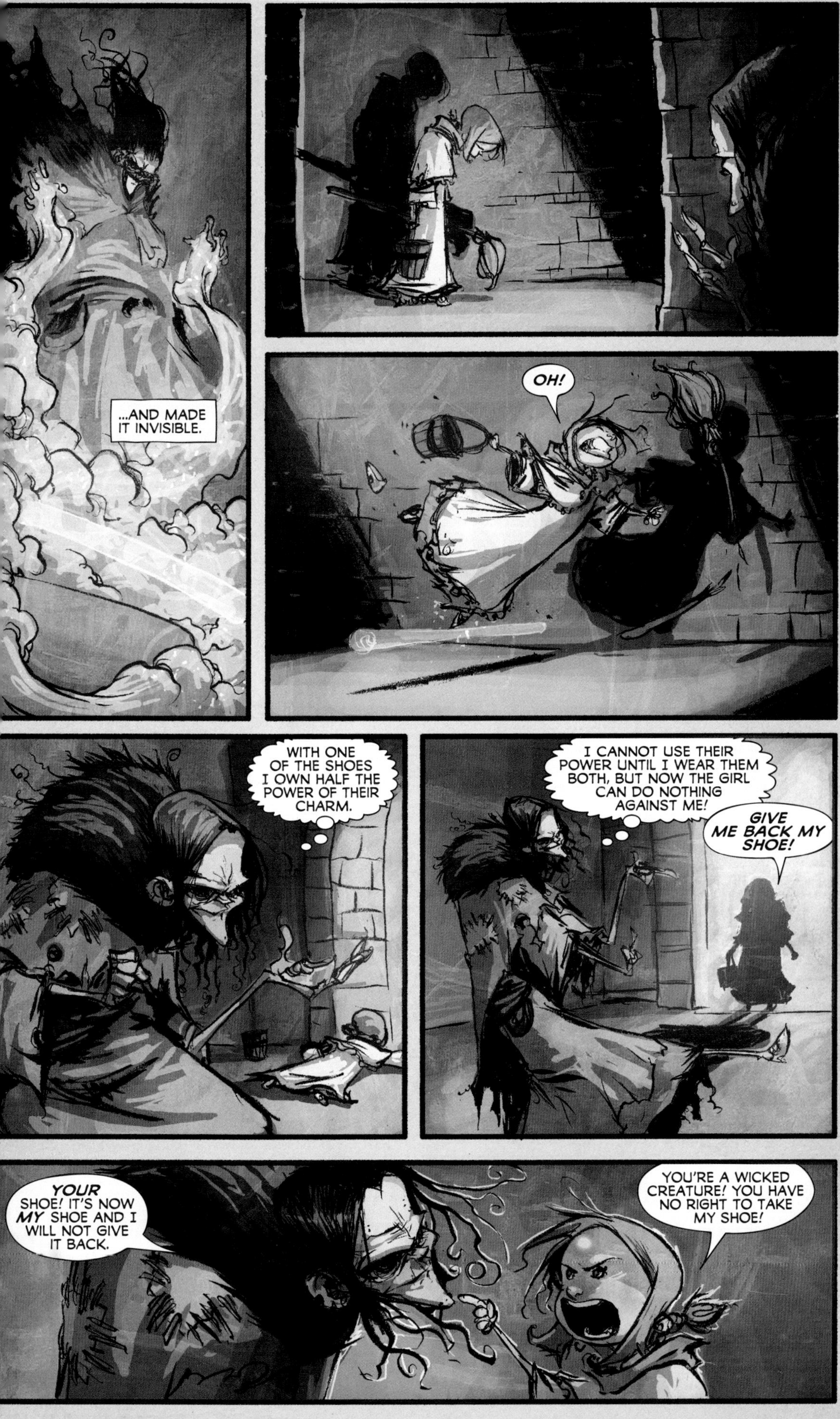
...AND MADE IT INVISIBLE.
OH!
WITH ONE OF THE SHOES I OWN HALF THE POWER OF THEIR CHARM.
I CANNOT USE THEIR POWER UNTIL I WEAR THEM BOTH, BUT NOW THE GIRL CAN DO NOTHING AGAINST ME!
GIVE ME BACK MY SHOE!
YOUR SHOE! IT'S NOW MY SHOE AND I WILL NOT GIVE IT BACK.
YOU'RE A WICKED CREATURE! YOU HAVE NO RIGHT TO TAKE MY SHOE!

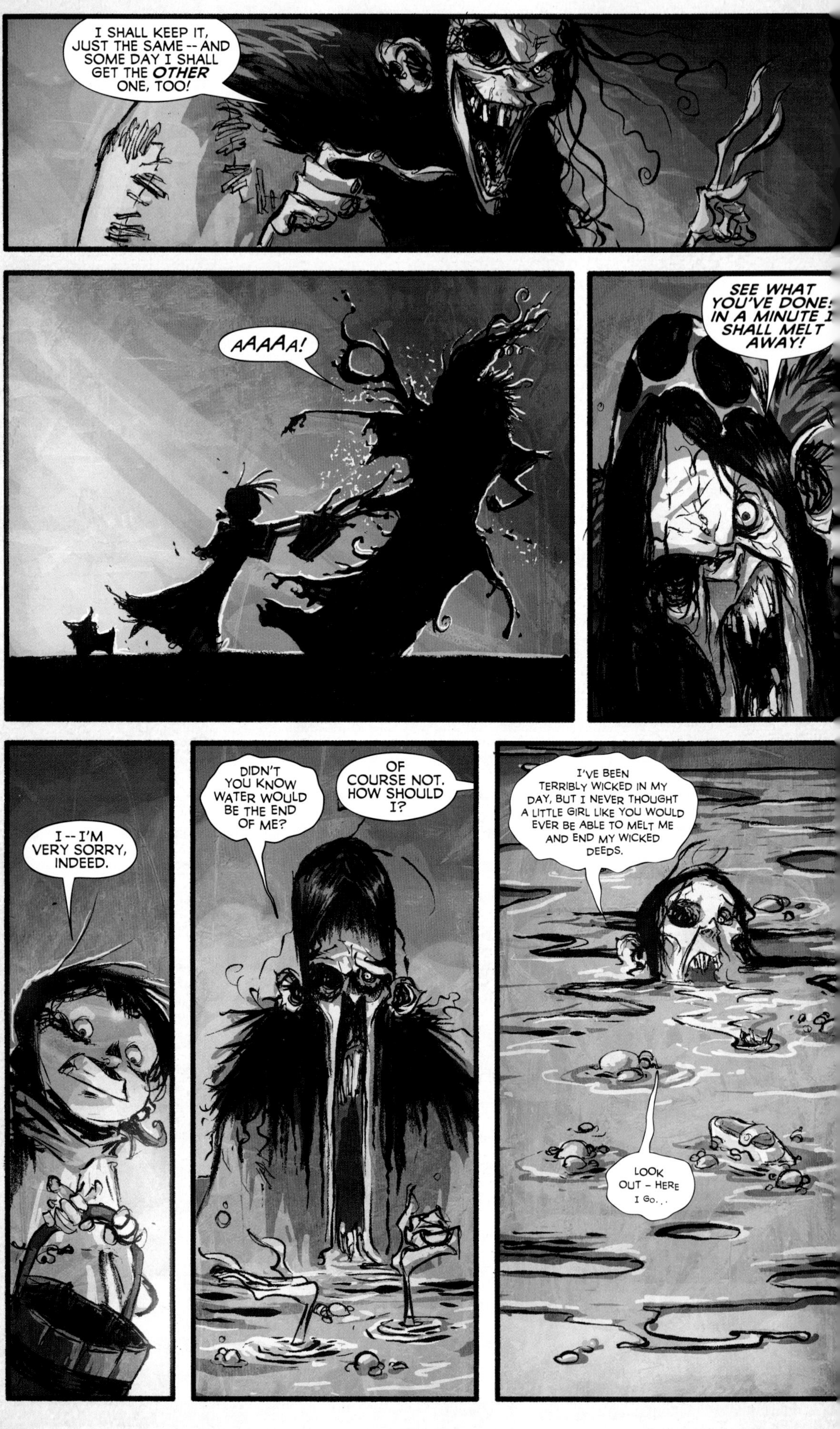
I SHALL KEEP IT, JUST THE SAME -- AND SOME DAY I SHALL GET THE *OTHER* ONE, TOO!
AAAAA!
SEE WHAT YOU'VE DONE! IN A MINUTE I SHALL MELT AWAY!
I -- I'M VERY SORRY, INDEED.
DIDN'T YOU KNOW WATER WOULD BE THE END OF ME?
OF COURSE NOT. HOW SHOULD I?
I'VE BEEN TERRIBLY WICKED IN MY DAY, BUT I NEVER THOUGHT A LITTLE GIRL LIKE YOU WOULD EVER BE ABLE TO MELT ME AND END MY WICKED DEEDS.
LOOK OUT - HERE I GO. . .

DOROTHY CLEANED AND DRIED THE SILVER SHOE, AND PUT IT ON HER FOOT AGAIN.

SEEING THAT THE WITCH HAD REALLY MELTED AWAY TO NOTHING, DOROTHY THREW ANOTHER BUCKET OF WATER OVER THE MESS, THEN SWEPT IT ALL OUT THE DOOR.

DOROTHY RAN OUT TO THE COURTYARD AND SET THE LION FREE.

THE WICKED WITCH OF THE WEST HAS COME TO AN END! WE'RE NO LONGER PRISONERS IN THIS STRANGE LAND!

I'M MUCH PLEASED TO HEAR THAT.

DOROTHY'S FIRST ACT WAS TO CALL ALL THE WINKIES TOGETHER. THERE WAS GREAT REJOICING AMONG THEM.

YOU ARE NO LONGER SLAVES!

IF THE SCARECROW AND TIN WOODMAN WERE ONLY WITH US, I SHOULD BE QUITE HAPPY.

DON'T YOU SUPPOSE WE COULD RESCUE THEM?

YOU'VE SET US FREE FROM BONDAGE.

WE'D BE DELIGHTED TO DO ALL IN OUR POWER TO HELP YOU.

*T*HEY TRAVELED THAT DAY AND PART OF THE NEXT TO THE ROCKY PLAIN WHERE THE TIN WOODMAN LAY.

CAN YOU STRAIGHTEN OUT THOSE DENTS, AND BEND HIM BACK INTO SHAPE, AND SOLDER HIM WHERE HE'S BROKEN?

SOME OF THE WINKIES WERE VERY GOOD TINSMITHS.

AFTER THREE DAYS AND FOUR NIGHTS --

THANK YOU FOR RESCUING ME.

IF WE ONLY HAD THE SCARECROW WITH US AGAIN, I SHOULD BE QUITE HAPPY.

WE MUST TRY TO FIND HIM.

THEY WALKED ALL THAT DAY AND PART OF THE NEXT UNTIL THEY CAME TO THE TALL TREE.

I'LL CHOP IT DOWN, AND THEN WE CAN GET THE SCARECROW'S CLOTHES.

CRASH·SH·SH

DOROTHY PICKED UP THE SCARECROW'S CLOTHES AND HAD THE WINKIES CARRY THEM BACK TO THE CASTLE.

THANK YOU, THANK YOU, MY FRIENDS.

THANK YOU FOR SAVING ME.

DOROTHY SPENT A FEW HAPPY DAYS AT THE YELLOW CASTLE. BUT ONE DAY SHE THOUGHT OF AUNT EM.

WE MUST GO BACK TO OZ AND CLAIM HIS PROMISE.

YES, AT LAST I SHALL GET MY BRAINS.

AND I SHALL GET MY COURAGE.

AND I SHALL GET MY HEART.

AND I SHALL GET BACK TO KANSAS!

LET'S START FOR THE EMERALD CITY TOMORROW!

THE NEXT DAY THEY CALLED THE WINKIES TOGETHER AND BADE THEM GOOD-BYE.

THE WINKIES BEGGED THE TIN WOODMAN TO STAY AND RULE OVER THEM.

BUT FINDING THEY WERE DETERMINED TO GO, THE WINKIES PRESENTED A GIFT TO EACH --

-- AND ALL SHOOK HANDS UNTIL THEIR ARMS ACHED.

DOROTHY WENT TO FILL HER BASKET WITH FOOD AND FOUND THE GOLDEN CAP.

SHE DIDN'T KNOW ANYTHING ABOUT ITS CHARM, BUT SHE SAW THAT IT WAS PRETTY, SO SHE MADE UP HER MIND TO WEAR IT.

THEN THEY STARTED FOR THE EMERALD CITY. THE WINKIES GAVE THEM THREE CHEERS AND MANY GOOD WISHES TO CARRY WITH THEM.